I'M FAST!

KATE & JIM McMULLAN

BALZER + BRAY
An Imprint of HarperCollinsPublishers

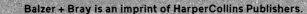

Balzer + Bray is an imprint of HarperCollins Publishers.

Library of Congress Cataloging-in-Publication Data.
McMullan, Kate.
       I'm fast! / by Kate & Jim McMullan. — 1st ed.
           p.   cm.
       Summary: A train and a car race each other to Chicago.
       ISBN 978-0-06-192085-1 (trade bdg.) — ISBN 978-0-06-192086-8 (lib. bdg.)
       [1. Railroad trains—Fiction.   2. Racing—Fiction.]   I. McMullan, Jim, ill.   II. Title.
III. Title: I am fast!
PZ7.M47879Il 2012   2010013669
[E]—dc22

12 13 14 15   SCP   10 9 8 7 6 5 4 ❖ First Edition

CHILDREN'S ROOM

For Anika & Carter Petruccelli

Thanks to the HarperCollins crew, Alessandra Balzer, Ruiko Tokunaga, Sara Sargent, Jenny Rozbruch, Carla Weise, and Kathryn Silsand, for keeping us ON TRACK, and a big TOOO-OOOO to Holly McGhee, Joan Slattery, and Elena Mechlin over at Pippin.

What's that, Red?
You wanna have a RACE?
Vrrrrrrrrrrr-rum!

First one to Chicago wins?
You're on!

Lemme load my FREIGHT.

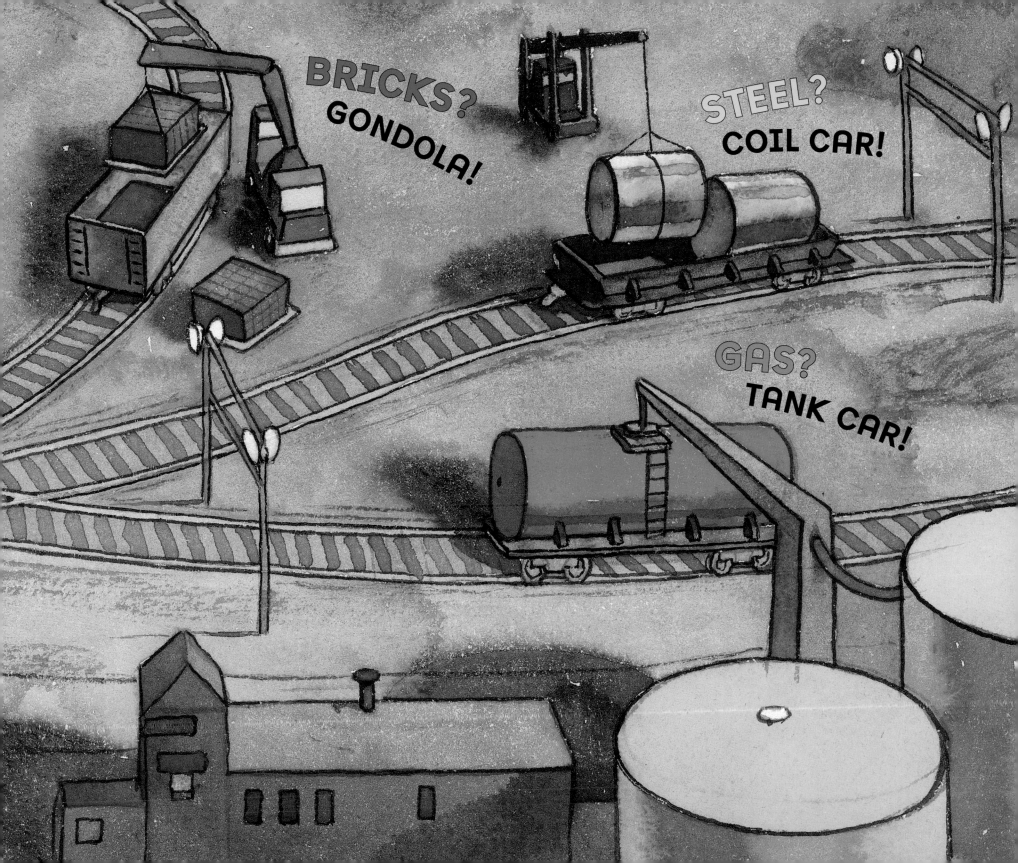

I'm haulin' a
FREEZER CAR full of
ICE-CREAM BARS!
Gotta get 'em to Chicago
ICY COLD!

Chooka chooka

chooka chooka

MOUNTAIN ahead!
CARS on my AUTO-RACK,
DUCK!

Takin' a shortcut
through the ROCK—

TOOOOOOOOOO-OO

Chooka chooka chooka chook

FULL SPEED AHEAD
through the tunnel—

TOOOOOOOOO!

Chooka chooka chooka chooka

Outta the DARK,
into the—

SNOW!

So? **PLOW** right through it.

Car? Can't do it—
Nothin' to it for a

FREIGHT TRAIN!

Choo-ka Choo-ka Choo-ka Choo-ka

I'm **EATIN' UP** track!

Got a **BOXCAR**
filled with **BOXES**—
filled with **WHEAT, EGGS,
TOMATOES, PEPPERS,**

CHEESE!

Chooka chooka chooka chooka

WHEELS on the RAILS, ALL night long,
Racin' and a-rumblin' the
FREIGHT TRAIN song—
Chooka chooka chooka chooka

Towin' TRUCKS—
STACKED PIGGYBACK!
TRUCKERS tucked inside
their cabs
SLEEP LIKE BABIES!

Shhhhhhhhh!

Chooka chooka chooka chooka

HOLY COW!

CATTLE on the TRACK!

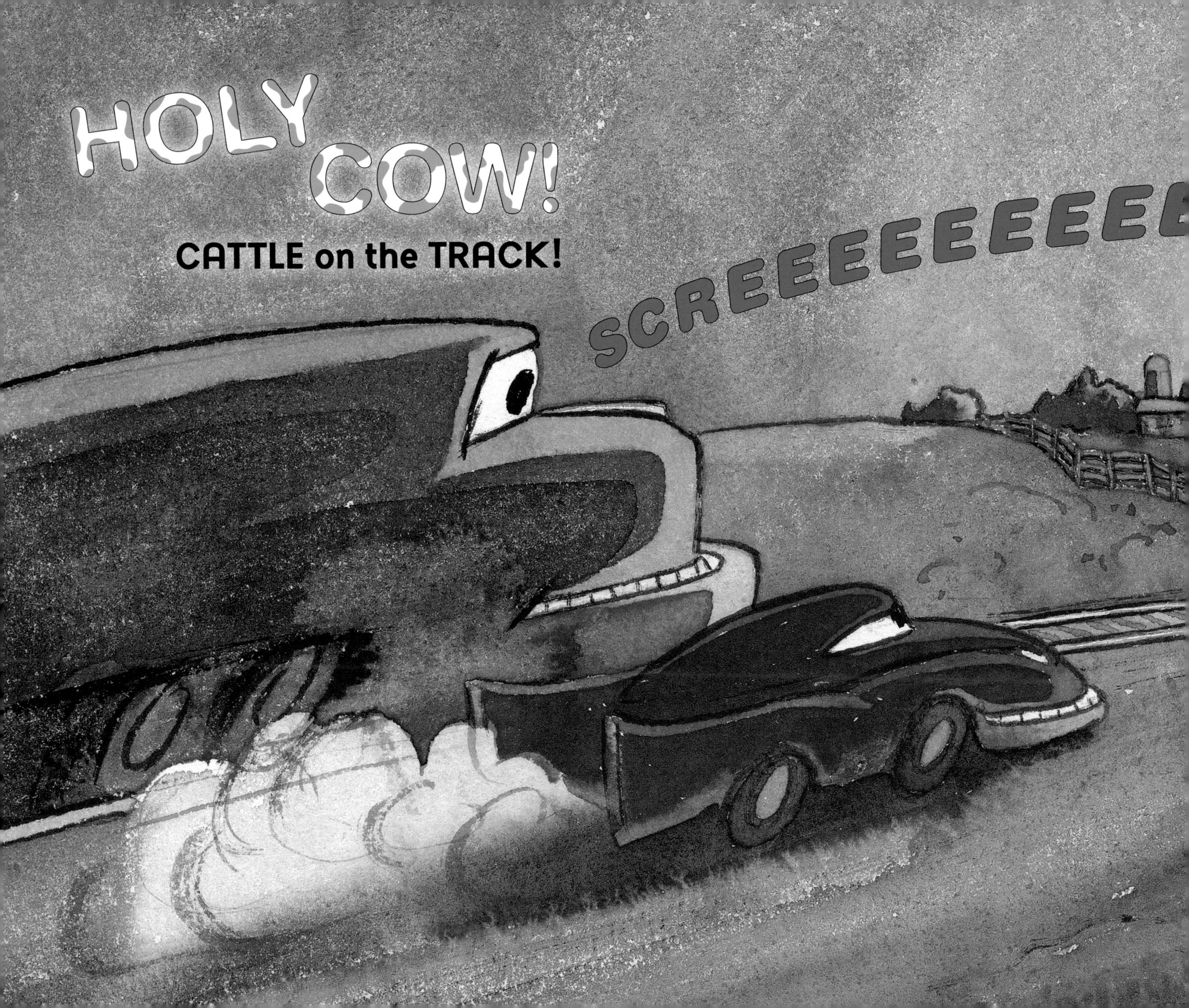

TOOOOOOOO-OO-OOOOOO!

Cows? You gotta *MOOOOOOOOVE* it!

Thanks, ladies!

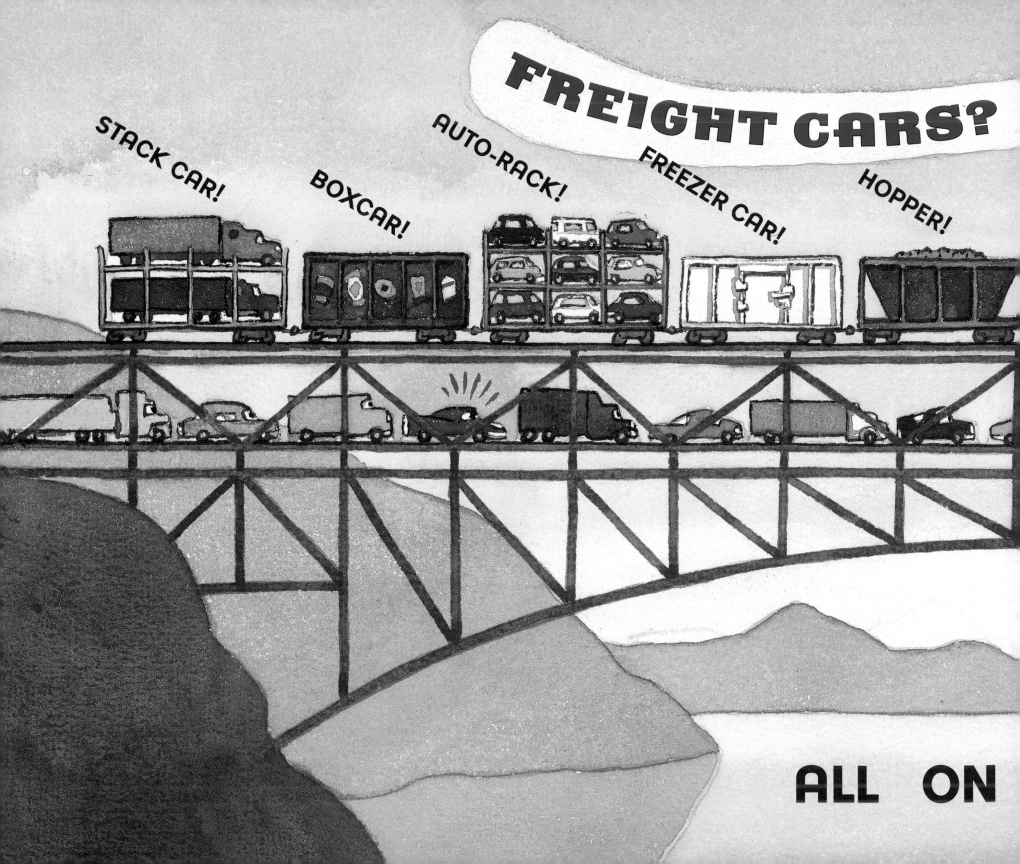

CLANG!
CLANG!
CLANG!
TOOOOOOO-OO-OOOOOOO!
Make WAY for the
FREIGHT TRAIN!

Onto the SIDE TRACK, THROTTLE BACK.

Won the race to Chicago—

YESSSSSSSSSSSSSSSSSSSSSSSSSSSSSS!

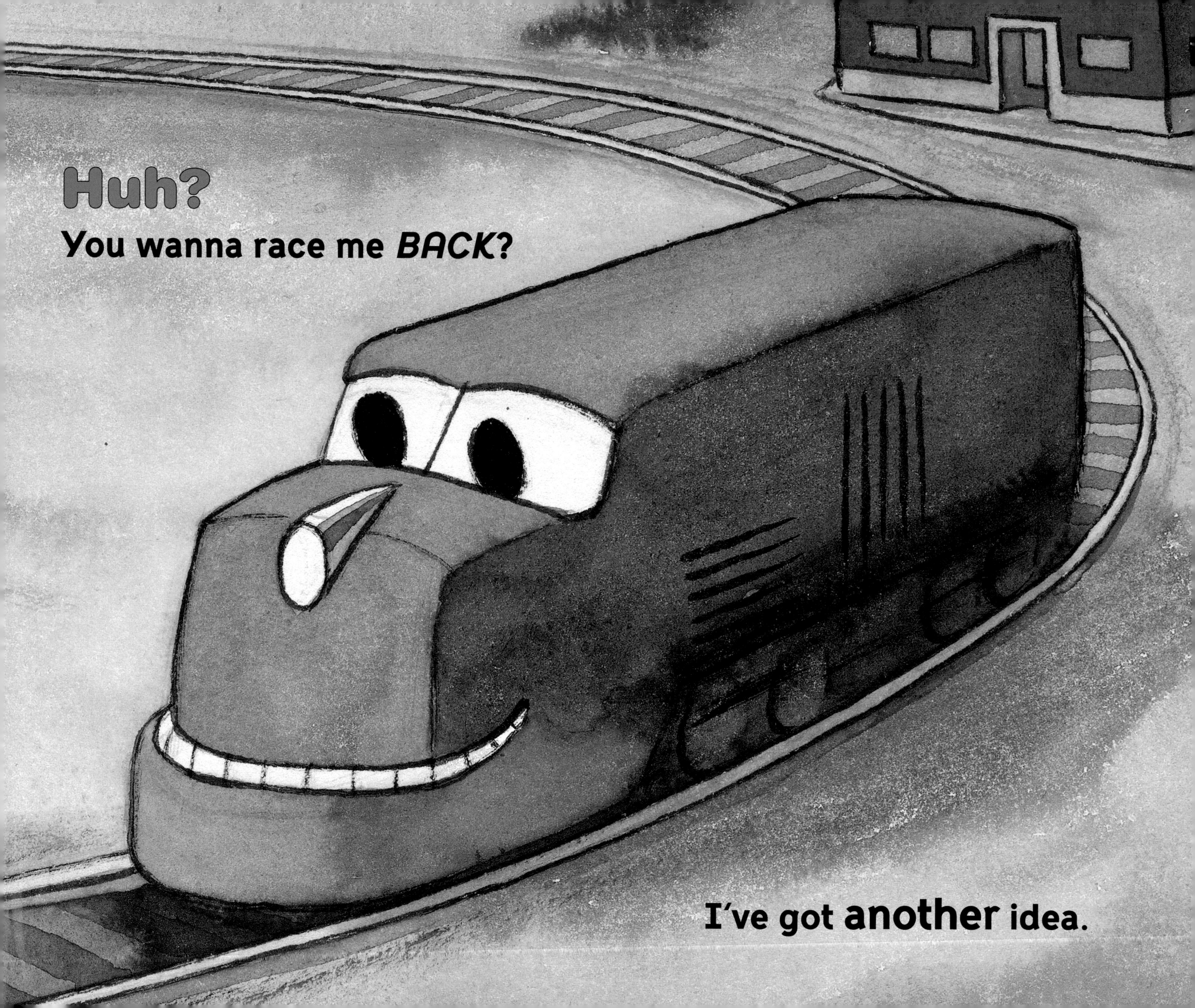

Huh?

You wanna race me *BACK*?

I've got another idea.

Take the **TRAIN**, Red!
Yeah, roll on up!
I'll get you there—

FAST!